BAOBAB PUBLISHING

PLANTING SEEDS OF CHARACTER, WISDOM, UNITY, AND LOVE

I0692403

Text and Illustrations Copyright © 2015 by Schertevear Q. Watkins
Address all inquiries to:
Baobab Books
Email: bbfbooks@gmail.com

ISBN-13:
978-0692549872 (Baobab Publishing)

ISBN-10:
0692549870

Characters Like Me

Characters Like Me is a series that celebrates diversity by showcasing main characters from different backgrounds and with unique qualities. While drawing on cultural backgrounds, these stories are relatable to all children.

The purpose of Characters Like Me is not to limit children to reading stories, only about characters that share their own characteristics. These books help children celebrate their individuality and value the differences in others. As a result, all the stories are based on topics that interest every child and family.

Characters Like Me

on

a and baobabpublishing.com

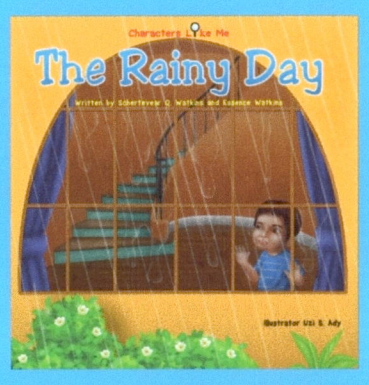

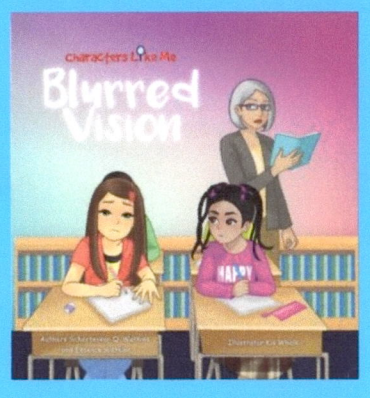

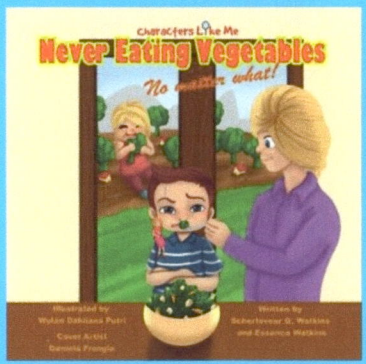

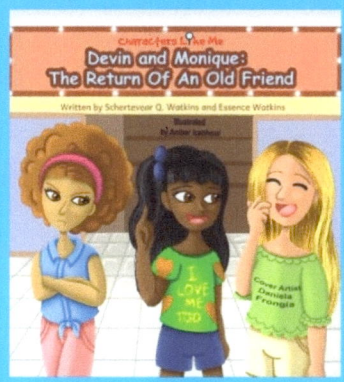

This Book Belongs To

_____

Chung was not like the other boys at his school or in his neighborhood. He was not into trucks, cars, video games, or bikes. Chung didn't find any of that interesting or intellectually stimulating. Because of this, the other boys didn't find him interesting either.

So, Chung concluded that it was best to make friends with something more welcoming and fascinating to him.

"Why worry about making friends with simplistic boys when there are all these amazing bugs," Chung thought.

Chung liked bugs because they were all different. They
all had special jobs to help keep the world flowing in
some way.

Everywhere Chung went he carried around his backpack, magnifying glass, and a
jar. Chung felt embarrassed when
the boys teased him at recess for putting a cockroach in a pickle jar.

"Cockroaches are important creatures," Chung explained
to the other boys. "Without cockroaches, the endangered
red-cockaded woodpecker would be no more."

But the boys didn't care to hear what Chung was saying. Instead, they laughed
and began throwing pinecones at Chung.

The other boys thought that Chung was strange for always hanging around and collecting bugs. They thought that people should hang with people and not creepy crawlers.

"Hey Bug Boy!" Anthony Willocks yelled out one day as he snatched Chung by the collar in the schoolyard. "Why don't you act like one of your bee friends and buzz off somewhere else."

All the other kids heard and laughed as Chung hung his head down in humiliation.

Recess was considered the worst time for Chung. None of the other boys wanted to play with him because he was different. Also, because Chung was different, he didn't want to play what the other boys were playing.

Chung didn't really mind not playing with the mean boys. But the mean boys felt that anyone that didn't like what they liked was odd. So, they picked on poor Chung every day on the playground.

The boys were so mean to Chung that one day as Chung collected lady bugs on the playground, Dao tripped Chung up and made him fall into a puddle of mud. Chung's jar flew right out of his hand and he lost his entire collection of lady bugs.

"Hey, now we get to see how chocolate covered lady bugs look," laughed Mason.

"Only it's not chocolate, Goofy," Cortez replied. "It's mud."

When Chung came home from school that evening, all his mother could see was mud stains all over Chung's brand new school uniform. This made Chung's mother very angry. She helped Chung clean up and they went right back up to the school. Mother had a serious talk with the teacher and principal regarding the boys who were bullying Chung on the playground.

That evening, when Chung and Mother got back from the school, Mother told Dad all about the incident on the playground. Dad tried to talk Chung into acting more like the other boys.

"Why don't you try playing video games or cars, and lay off the bugs for a while?" Dad suggested.

Mother didn't like the fact that Dad tried to persuade Chung to change in order to get along with the mean boys.

"Chung shouldn't have to change to make others happy," Mother expressed.

That night, when Chung went to sleep,
he dreamt that
he was a giant wasp. In this dream,
Chung stung all the mean boys who
teased and bullied him on the
playground.

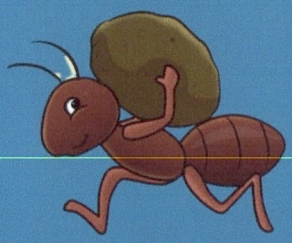

The next day at recess, Dao came up to Chung and yelled at him for getting him into trouble. "You better not blab to your mom about me again!" Dao threatened.

"Leave him alone or I'll tell then," Ying warned as she stood next to a tree, listening to Chung and Dao's conversation.

Dao knew that Ying meant business and decided to leave Chung alone for the rest of the day.

Ying was always watching when the other boys teased Chung. Ying was different too, just like Chung. She never played with the other girls. Instead, she always spent her recess time reading books. She would read books about gardens. Ying's mother owned a flower shop.

"You know plants and bugs are linked," Ying said, smiling at Chung.

One day at school, Ying stopped Chung in the hallway. "Do you mind if I walk to class with you?" Ying asked.

Chung didn't know how to respond to Ying's friendliness and smiles. The only way Chung knew to respond was to clam up and say nothing. But then Ying took a book out of her backpack. The book was called, "Worms, the Undercover Gardeners."

Ying extended the book out for Chung to take and said, "It's all about how worms help prepare the soil for plants to grow, along with other worm facts. You can keep it until Monday."

That weekend, Chung read all about worms. It was the greatest book that Chung had ever read, especially the part that said that there was a worm that grew to 22ft.

"Ying must like bugs too," Chung's mother said.

Chung thought about it for a second and then concluded
that his mother might be right. Not in a million years did Chung ever
consider that anyone else would ever think
like him, especially a girl.

"What should I do now?" Chung questioned.

"What do you think you should do?" Mother asked.
"Who is this Ying girl that gave you the worm book?"

Mother had seen Ying's name in the book when she
moved it off Chung's bed Saturday night. Chung told
his mother about Ying and how she took up for him.
Mother suggested that they should become friends.

Monday at recess Chung returned the book to Ying. Then Chung asked Ying if she wanted to watch the ant hills with him. Ying agreed and they talked about ants all during recess.

"Did you know that ants have wars and the winning colony may keep prisoners from the defeated colony to work as their slaves?" Ying asked.

"Yeah, and did you know that ants are very strong? If we were as strong as an ant we would be able to lift our parents' cars," Chung shared.

Although Ying had been known as a loner, just as Chung had the other kids never teased Ying. Unlike Chung, Ying carried herself with confidence. She didn't care if the other girls thought she was dull or weird.

All Ying knew is that no matter how much they stared or whispered, no one better utter any words of disrespect to her face. And no one on the playground dared to.

Everyday Chung and Ying sat together at lunch, played during recess and walked home together. Now that Chung and Ying hung with each other, neither of them were considered loners.

The mean boys no longer bothered Chung and the girls who never bothered to speak to Ying, would always speak now when she passed by.

Chung and Ying would sometimes play in one another's yards. When Chung came to Ying's house, he would help her do her chores in her mother's flower garden. Ying only lived four houses down.

They became best friends. Chung had finally found someone who was as different and intellectually stimulating as he.

Thinking Questions

1. Why was Mother upset by what Dad said to Chung?
2. What did Chung and Ying have in common?
3. Why do you think the children treated both Chung and Ying differently after they became friends with one another?

Recalling The Events

1. Where at school was Chung on the days he was teased in this story?
2. Why did Chung decide that collecting bugs was better than hanging out with the other boys?
3. What did Ying loan to Chung in the hallway at school?
4. What or who stopped the bullies in this story?

More About The Story

1. What is the name of this book?
2. Who is the Authors and/or Illustrator?
3. Who is the main character in this story?
4. What is the mood of the main character? Why does he feel this way?
5. Does the main character resolve his problem in the end? If so, how is the problem resolved?
6. What does the Author want children to learn when they read or hear this story?
7. What is your opinion about the main character's problem and how it was solved?

Anthony CHUNG CORTEZ Ying Dao Mason

HELP STOP BULLYING

1. Don't be an audience. Bullies love to show off the mean things they do.
2. Befriend the person who is being bullied.
3. Tell a trusting adult if you or someone you know is being bullied.
4. Don't spread or share messages that will hurt someone's feelings.
5. Never tease, spread rumors or hurt someone just because they are different.
6. Always remember that **EVERYONE WAS CREATED SPECIAL AND UNIQUE.**

Follow the author.

Don't forget to
REVIEW

amazon

www.ingramcontent.com/pod-product-compliance
Lightning Source LLC
Chambersburg PA
CBHW041540240626
47164CB00002B/75